D1344928

50000000004699

For Jason, my forever friend
~CF
For Anna, with all my love
~BC

Text Copyright © 2007 by Claire Freedman
Illustration Copyright © 2007 by Ben Cort
Published by arrangement with Simon & Schuster UK Ltd
1st Floor, 222 Gray's Inn Road, London, WC1X 8HB
A CBS Company

Dual language text copyright © 2011 Mantra Lingua
Audio copyright © 2011 Mantra Lingua
A CIP record for this book is available from the British Library
Mantra Lingua, Global House, 303 Ballards Lane, London, N12 8NP

www.mantralingua.com

All rights reserved. No part of this book may be reproduced or transmitted in any form
or by any means, electronic or mechanical, including photocopying, recording or by any
information storage and retrieval system without permission in writing from the Publisher.
Printed in Hatfield,UK FP300612PB08127145

Hear each page of this talking book narrated in many languages
with TalkingPEN! Then record your own versions.

Touch the arrow below with the TalkingPEN to start

Start   Info   English   Language

Ateiviams patinka kelnaitės
Aliens Love Underpants

Claire Freedman & Ben Cort

Lithuanian translation by Deimante Dambrauskiene

Mantra Lingua

Ateiviai garbina kelnaitės
Nesvarbu dydis, forma ar spalva
Tik štai kur didelė bėda –
Kelnaičių kosmose nėra…

Aliens love underpants,
Of every shape and size.
But there are no underpants in space,
So here's a big surprise…

Kai ateiviai išsiruošia Žemėn,
Jie skrenda ne pas TAVE…
Jie atvyksta čia tavo kelnaičių
Spėju to nežinojai, ar ne?

When aliens fly down to Earth, they don't come to meet YOU...
They simply want your underpants - I'll bet you never knew!

Štai erdvėlaivio žybsi radaras
Ir skleidžia visokius garsus.
Vos pamato kedenamus vėjo,
Išdžiaustytus apatinius.

Their spaceship's radar bleeps and blinks the moment that it sees
A washing line of underpants all flapping in the breeze.

Nes jie sveteliai nekviesti
Jie nutupia sodely.
O-o-o, KELNAITĖS! – skanduoja, šoka
Jie linksmai ir džiaugiasi be galo.

They land in your back garden, though they haven't been invited.
"Oooooh, UNDERPANTS!" they chant, and dance around, delighted.

Patinka raudoni, patinka žali,
Oranžiniai kaip apelsinai,
Bet ypatingai žavi juos visus
Taškuoti močiutės apatiniai.

They like them red, they like them green, or orange like satsumas.
But best of all they love the sight of Granny's spotted bloomers.

Tikrai puiki vietelė slėptis
Mamos kelnaitės puošnios
Vilnoniais bočiaus apatiniais
Labai smagu nučiuožti.

Mum's pink frilly knickers are a perfect place to hide
And Grandpa's woolly longjohns make a super-whizzy slide.

In daring competitions, held up by just one peg,
They count how many aliens can squeeze inside each leg.

Bebaimėse varžybose
Jie dalyvaut ketina.
Skaičiuoja kiek ateivių tilps
Į vienus apatinius?

Atrodo juokingai ateiviai visi
Varžyboms keistom pasiruošę.
Apatiniai ant kojų, galvų užmauti,
Net erdvėlaivis jais pasipuošęs.

They wear pants on their feet and heads and other silly places.
They fly pants from their spaceships and hold Upside-Down-Pant Races!

Ateiviams išmonės netrūksta,
Linksmybių jiems visiems apstu,
Kai jie elastines kelnaites
Padaro savo batutu.

As they go zinging through the air,
it really is pants-tastic.
What fun the aliens can have
with pingy pants elastic!

Tai ne išdykęs paikas šuo
Ar pokštauja kaimynai.
ATEIVIUS kaltinti turi
Kai dingsta apatiniai.

It's not your neighbour's naughty dog, or next-door's funny game.
When underpants go missing, the ALIENS are to blame!

But quick! Mum's coming out to fetch the washing in at last.
Wheee! Off the aliens all zoom, they're used to leaving fast...

Greičiau, ateiviai, paskubėkit!
Mama ateina skalbinių.
Išskrist tolyn nepastebėtiems
Jums neturėtų būt sunku.

Kai maunies išskalbtas kelnaitės
Prieš tai gerai patikrink jas.
Juk ką žinai, gal koks ateivis
Dar tebetūno viduje!

So when you put your pants on, freshly washed and nice and clean,
Just check in case an alien still lurks inside, unseen!